HUNDRED ACRE

— 0 —

three criminal elements by
Doug Lane

midnight-to-three publishing

2023

for
MARY STEPHENS,
to whom I can honestly say, à la Milne,
"When we were very young,"
and have it be
True

Illustrations for "Hundred Acre" by the author, after the style of and incorporating elements created by E.H. Shepard for the first edition of WINNIE THE POOH by A.A. Milne, first published in the United States in 1926, and which entered the public domain in the United States of America in 2022.

Published by Midnight-To-Three Publishing, Salem, OR
MTT-002

ISBN: 978-0-9895417-6-3 (paperback)

First Edition

DOING THE CRIME

There are many truths about publishing. The one underpinning this small folio of murder, mayhem, and heroics is this: in 2022, there are only a handful of pro-paying mystery or crime markets left. Compare to the 40s and 50s, when the newsstands were full of nifty puzzles, gun play, and gristle, and dozens of outlets needed gumshoes, thugs, and peril to cram between covers.

A few remain. Ellery Queen's Mystery Magazine is probably the standard-bearer now, though Alfred Hitchcock's is still around. The Strand, whose ancestor attended the birth and rise of Arthur Conan Doyle and his resident of 221B Baker Street, persists but is almost impossible to find on a newsstand. There are others, but they fill up quickly when opened for submissions. If it's funny there are so few magazines serving the genre, it's at a time when the mystery novel flourishes, continuing to rouse readers with the age-old, single-word question: whodunit? And readers are still eating it up - old, new, hard-boiled, locked room, anti-hero, on and on. Maybe mystery readers simply want the banquet over the bread stick.

The first two stories herein made the rounds of the major magazines in the field, and they both rolled snake eyes over and over. I blame the fact they're not straight-up mysteries: one is a perversion of children's literature; the other, a stew of fantasy and crime. I enjoyed cooking them up too much to pitch them to the penny-a-word (or less) editorial crowd or leave them on ice until the next collection. Pennies? I can mint my own, thanks. And this being a DIY stint, I've rounded things out with the return of an old superhero friend. (Yes, kids - *he's* back.)

Welcome to the rogues gallery. I hope you have as much fun walking through it as I've had setting it up.

Doug Lane
Salem, OR
11/15/22

Who doesn't love cramming chocolate into peanut butter? SF mysteries. Horror comedies. Fictional memoir. Our first tale runs along the mashup line: take the private investigative milieu and whip it together with a legendary children's book. As the cover letter put it to editors, "Is this a satire of the hard-boiled tradition? A commentary on the perils of the public domain? A crowbar to our collective childhood?" To be honest. I still don't know. And further, as a cranky old Jew I knew was fond of saying, deponent sayeth not.

Hundred Acre

1

Christopher Robin was dead.

He hadn't gone without a fight. His jacket offered silent testimony, tattered strips stained in the pool of his blood. Whoever'd worked him over did so in a rage. Big bruises. Broken bones. He was slumped face-down in the grass near the banquet table in the clearing, his small hands balled into fists. He hadn't had enough in the tank to hold off whoever'd done the deed.

Roo had found him, the poor kid. He cowered now at the bottom of his mom's pouch, his shrieks still audible even through her skin and over the noise of Hundred Acre. He'd never unsee it. Two bits of crushed innocence for the price of one. Kanga rubbed the outside of her pouch with a gentleness belying the violence of the scene. "He was so kind to us. Who could do this? Why?"

"I don't know, Kanga. But I'm going to find out."

"You?" Her glance was confusion, her voice doubt. "Humans have authorities who do this for a living, Pooh. They're far better suited to look into it than any of us."

"You're probably right. It's an awful lot for one bear to think about." I tapped my forehead for effect. Kanga's gaze softened. Good. I'd worked my whole life to set low expectations. Letting them all believe I was a bumbler with little brain had allowed me to glide under the radar this long. Silly? Often. Old? Certainly.

Bear? By design of pattern and stitch of thread. And I planned to snap closed like a grizzly on the throat of the person who'd murdered my friend.

2

It was a beautiful pencil case. Japanese Paulownia, ebony stain. Nothing like that wood grew in the forest. I imagined wherever Christopher Robin found it in the world beyond Hundred Acre was an exotic place: Buddhas carved from marble and bright paper lanterns and candles and such. I still remember the day he gave it to me. He threw me a party for saving Piglet during the flood. I told him I didn't have pencils for it.

"You'll figure out its purpose," he told me and gave me a rub between the ears. Bother. I was going to miss the head scratches.

In the end, he was right. I used it to hold clues. None of the usual suspects knew I solved mysteries. A hundred acres is a lot of real estate, rife with intrigue beyond our small corner. Crows, squirrels, snakes, those pain-in-the-ass beavers–there were dozens of creatures who had their problems and could pay their honeypots. The name I used on my card matched the sign over my door: Mr. Sanders. When in doubt, hide in plain sight. I glanced up at the sign, the letters old, deeply cut in the board. Someday I'll solve the mystery of who the hell Sanders was.

Today the box held the pictures. Waiting Kanga out was hard. I finally convinced her to fetch Owl while I kept an eye on the scene. It was harder to point the camera. I didn't want to remember Christopher Robin that way, but I knew what would happen. There was now police tape where his small boy's body was found. The men in blue had removed it, left a thousand footprints in the dirt. Scene ruined. Nothing more to see there. Before then, I took over two-dozen images. Once I knew who'd killed him, I was going to cram as many as I could down their throat and burn the rest.

The dry twigs I spread across the lane to my tree announced a visitor. I tucked the pencil box under my chair and crammed my maw into a convenient honey pot. Thirty seconds later, Rabbit rounded the bend in the path. Word had circulated. His shakes were bad for someone who didn't drink. He appeared old, skinny. I was probably seeing him through the filter of current events. He asked if he could sit.

"Of course, Rabbit." I pushed the pot at him. "Honey?"

His exasperation was bottomless. You'd think I'd offered him rabbit stew. "How can you eat at a time like this?"

"One should never be sad on an empty stomach." I was smacking my lips when he grabbed the pot from me and threw it against my door with a strangled cry. It takes some force to shatter a pot full of honey. The larger pieces of crockery fell to the ground. Golden rivulets oozed down the door, carrying the shards. Bother. I was going to need more ant traps.

Rabbit kicked another pot and it sailed into the tree line. "You're impossible! You thoughtless, witless, heartless excuse for a bear! Don't you even *care* who did this?"

The 'who' was a problem. Or maybe the 'whom'. I never get that one right. But the scene of the crime was its own first clue: a place Christopher Robin knew, somewhere he felt safe. His guard was down. The killer wasn't someone from some other part of Hundred Acre, a pissed off moose or other opportunist who'd crossed the river into our neck to batter a random stranger. It had to have been one of us.

I'd ruled out Roo immediately, less because he discovered

the scene than because of his small stature. Similarly, Piglet was smaller than Christopher Robin and meek. From there, suspects became a crapshoot. Four other residents of Hundred Acre had the physical means. Kanga was all legs. So was Eeyore, if he wasn't navel-gazing. A beating wasn't Owl's M.O.– he was claws and carnage–but the strength was there.

And Rabbit had a temper. No revelation there–ask my honeypots. He seemed overwrought in the aftermath of what had happened, but the physicality of his outburst wasn't lost on me. At the end of most days, he seemed like so much wind in a sock. But everyone thought I was dumb as rocks with a head full of fluff. Who's to say we all weren't playing roles?

Still, he wasn't my first suspect. I had a different idea. And a lifetime of experience informed me the worst thing you could do was share an idea with Rabbit. Couldn't button his lip to keep his foot from becoming a keychain. If I was wrong, Rabbit would still be in his sad little warren after, but I needed him to leave so I could chase down my lead.

Piglet told me once if Rabbit was Saint Francis, I could have driven him to beat his dog. I swung that skill like a club. "I wonder if the Honeybee swarm could have done this."

"The... the Honeybee swarm?"

"Oh yes, Rabbit. They've always been trouble of one kind or another."

He blinked those weird rabbit eyes at me. "Did you *see* him?"

"Him who?"

"Christopher Robin!"

"Oh yes. It was horrible. I think I may have already repressed the memory."

The exasperation came roaring back. "Did you see *any sort* of bee sting on him?"

"Bee sting? Oh, no. I've had enough of those in the pursuit of honey, I think I'd have recognized bee stings." I paused and put on a vacant stare. "Mmmmmm. Honey."

Six shots in the 10 ring. Rabbit couldn't have looked madder if foam had come out with the spittle. He sputtered and stuttered and finally stormed away down the path, leaving me alone with my idea.

No one came calling at my tree after nightfall. You'd figure Owl might, but a little-known fact about our feathered friend is he's terrified of the dark. The rest probably pegged me for a sugar crash by nine. It made it easy for me to slip out under cover of dark.

He lived in a cave at the far edge of our part of Hundred Acre, uphill from Murky Lake. I'd tracked him there a long time ago. Tried to trap him. It went as well as you imagine. I never thought I'd be dumb enough or desperate enough to go calling. What we considered mutual respect was as sturdy as tissue paper, and if he was the killer, I had no way when I confronted him to prevent receipt of the same beating as Christopher Robin got.

I shouted into the cave. "Heffalump. Drag your wrinkled carcass out here."

He bellowed. Shambled. A light came on above the mouth of the cave. I wondered who he got to install that. He stopped shy of the opening, but there was enough glow to see him. He was gristle with tusks. Rheumy eyes. I wondered if his trunk was still handy with a blade. He looked me up and down, maybe sizing me for a coffin, maybe a meal. Who the hell knows what goes on in a Heffalump's head? "Sanders. Or do you still go by Poop?"

"It's Pooh. But you know that, so let's cut the antagonistic BS."

He snorted. "You're a long way from your den, bear."

"It's like the old proverb about Mohammed and the mountain. You sure as hell weren't coming to me."

Confusion. "Which one am I in this metaphor?"

"The stupid one. It's a wonder an ivory poacher hasn't smothered you with a pillow yet."

He stepped into the halo of light and cracked the knuckles on both of his front feet. "This is a lot of effort to get stomped."

"Like Christopher Robin?"

You can read a person's truth through the windows of their eyes. Especially when you throw a rock through them. Heffalump had heard. Maybe a little bird, maybe a big one. Hundred Acre

needed a town crier like Owl the way it needed clear-cutting. The Heffalump knew what had been done, but he hadn't done it. He came by the sorrow on his wrinkled gray face honestly. Ever see a Heffalump cry? First time for me. "He was a sweet child. Carefree. So imaginative. Sometimes, he came out here just to make sure I was taking care of myself."

I didn't let my surprise show. "That's who he was."

"He named me, you know."

"To be honest, I didn't."

He realized then why I was there. Frowned. "Do you really think I'm capable of something this horrible?"

"You have feet like concrete and know how to throw them. It fit the crime. Made you the easiest box to tick off first."

His sigh was an anvil. "I'm a Heffalump. Not a monster."

There was nothing to say to make it better. I didn't try.

"I'm sorry for your loss."

I scuffed a foot in the dirt. "Thank you. Though I suppose it's *our* loss." The silence grew uncomfortable. "I'll see myself out," I said, even though I'd never actually been in.

I'd gone a dozen steps, thinking about how to tangle with Rabbit next, when Heffalump called after me. "Pooh?"

"Yes?"

"If you discover who did this, bring them here and leave them at my door. Five minutes. I'll make it worth your while."

A glance back told me the Heffalump meant it to his bones. Funny when revenge is the common tongue. "There's not enough honey in the world to buy my spot in line, saggy-baggy. But if I need someone to hold the bastard down while I work, you're top of the list."

He nodded, massive ears flapping as he did, entered his cave, and turned out his light.

4

The next morning over toast with honey and jam, I studied the photos pixel by pixel. Reliving my broken friend in still form was fresh trauma. I was glad I'd never taken to mead–I'd have been even more useless than I already felt.

Rabbit wasn't my only hopping suspect. He had local kin. I hadn't ruled them out either. I scoured each frame for any sign of a rabbit track: whole, partial, even a toe. But if there were tracks, they eluded me. The edges of the pictures were getting sticky–napkins never seem to get onto the shopping list–when I noticed what my Lepus bias led me to stare past once, twice, thrice: straw. Strands of it pressed in the mud and stuck in blood on the sole of Christopher Robin's left shoe.

There wasn't anything straw or straw-like in the clearing. It was late spring. Natural straw was still months away. Rabbit lived in a warren, your basic dirt burrow. No straw to track from there to the clearing.

I needed a better look, so I went back to the scene. The beauty of cultivating an image of ignorance is deniability if asked why you ignored the police tape. I found the strands I'd photographed, trampled by police but still evident. Turned a couple in my hand. Close-up, it wasn't even straw from a bale or field. It was cleaned, processed. The kind one found in a broom.

We didn't keep a broom in the clearing. Anyone knows you don't sweep a forest. But if you used a broom handle as a weapon, straw could certainly come loose in the struggle. Especially one so violent.

Orderly creatures kept cleaning implements. One glance through my front door and you'd believe I couldn't even spell 'broom'. But I knew one methodically clean animal in our part of the forest, despite the old saying. And he owned a broom.

I stared at the thin strands, a small clue doubling as a neon red arrow tall as the hundred-year-old oak where the equally small and impossible suspect made his home.

5

Sometimes you want to reject reality. Make-believe is much more grand. Nothing goes wrong, the cupboard is always full, there are never little black rain clouds, and none of your friends would ever maim or kill any of your other friends. But the reality of what happened to Christopher Robin was unyielding. As I walked the lane to Piglet's door, honeypot in my hand, I wasn't sure what form justice would take.

Piglet lived in a tree—why was as big a mystery as the broken board out front of it with TRESPASSERS W- painted on what remained. Piglet had some stock tale about how it was his grandfather's name. I hadn't yet figured out Mr. Sanders, but I'd found the rest of Piglet's sign down by the riverbank the summer after the flood. I hadn't the heart to tell him his grandfather's last name probably wasn't WILL BE SHOT.

I rang the brass bell hanging outside his door. A call came from behind the tree. I followed the foot-worn path around the trunk to the back yard.

Piglet was on the small deck he'd added awhile back for

entertaining. He tipped a battered watering can, making it rain on potted flowers. No idea what kind; my knowledge of flowers stopped at their colors. He glanced up from gardening, set the can aside. "Oh, Pooh! How are you?"

"About as well as can be expected." The deck appeared oddly unkempt. "How are you?"

"Oh, keeping busy. Trying not to think about troubling things." He noticed the honeypot tucked in the crook of my left arm. "I'm sorry. Were we having lunch today?"

"This? Oh, no. I was just out walking, and I didn't want to go without a smackerel, in case my mind wandered and my feet followed. You know how it is."

"Yes, of course." He fidgeted. "This business with Christopher Robin is terrifying. Something like that, right here."

"I know. It's hard to fathom." How long had I known Piglet? It seemed forever. I didn't believe him capable of the deed, and still: small, timid, unassuming. If a monster wanted to dwell among us, was there a better way to hide? "I was wondering, Piglet, if I might borrow your broom."

"My... my broom?"

"Yes. I'm afraid my clutter had become a bit clutter-y of late. I should like to sweep some of it away before it decides to fall on me."

He nodded. "That makes sense."

"So, your broom. Might I borrow it?"

"Well, certainly you could if I had one. That is to say, still had one. I'm afraid I'm between brooms at the moment."

My hackles rose. "Between brooms?"

"Yes. My broom was broken recently. Someone was careless with it." He moved for the watering can.

Before he could reach it, I leapt at him and knocked him to the deck. He let out an "Oof!" when I landed on him. He was no match for me. He struggled until I smacked the honeypot into the deck beside his head. The resounding clunk made him a small Piglet statue. "Pooh, what are you doing?"

My voice was a cold blade. "Out of deference to our friendship, I'm giving you thirty seconds to admit what you did and explain yourself. If I don't like your explanation, I'm going to work you over, starting with that yellow belly of yours." I thudded the jar next to his head again for emphasis. "Go."

I expected a cry for help no one would hear. He went the other way, fat tears welling in his little pig eyes. "I'm sorry, Pooh! I'm so sorry! I couldn't help myself! If I could take it back, I would!"

I fought the urge to wrap my mitten-shaped paws around his windpipe. "Say his name."

"Wha-wha-what?"

"If you're going to confess, you say his name!"

He blubbered and spit and nodded. He choked on sounds trying to get them out before blurting, "Honey pot 16!"

Time and space seized like a dry engine. "What did you say?"

"Hi-hi-his name. Honey p-p-pot 16. That's what you'd written on it. I know it was wrong, but I came calling and you weren't home, and I realized I had nothing in the cupboard, and it was a long walk home, and you had *so* many jars and pots and barrels. The one I took was on a low shelf, behind so many others, and I planned to fill it again before I returned it, and then this whole terrible thing with Christopher Robin happened, and–"

"Christ, Piglet. Shut up for a minute."

He wailed. "It's just honey!"

I slapped him across the jowl. "Your broom. What happened to it?"

"It was broken. It came unstrung. It fell apart right after I got it back."

"You said someone was careless with it. Who?"

"I don't understand. I thought this was about the honey I took."

I was about to slap him again to focus him when I heard the voice beside us. "I'm sorry to interrupt. No one answered the front bell."

We both turned. I'd been so focused on Piglet I hadn't even heard the donkey enter the yard. "Good morning, Eeyore."

His voice was slow, maybe bored. Like always. "Pooh. Piglet. I heard a commotion. I don't tend to look for trouble, but it sure seems to find me. Kind of like you finding my tail, Pooh. Thanks again for that."

"It's really my fault," Piglet told him. "I took some of Pooh's honey and it seems to have snowballed into a great misunderstanding. Like with you and the broom that got broken."

I turned in time for Eeyore's back hooves to put out my lights.

6

The odor of stable ushered back my senses. Dirt, dung, straw, damp. My head throbbed. It was already end of the day, the horizon a fiery tapestry.

I'd never visited Eeyore's stable before, even when I found his missing tail doubling for Owl's bell rope. We always seemed to meet on mutual territory, in the clearing or elsewhere around Hundred Acre. I hadn't missed much. The stable was a half-dozen termites and a blustery day from falling down.

He'd tied my wrists behind a post. I'd gotten off easier than Piglet, who'd been unironically hog tied. It appeared pork was on the donkey's menu: a fire pit beyond the stable entrance was rigged with a spit, awaiting only flame and a trussed roast.

I glanced around the space. There were as many empty prescription bottles as I had honeypots. I'm not sure if Eeyore had a habit and was stoned senseless, or had run out of antidepressants and broken his brain by quitting cold. I'm not sure it mattered in either case.

Eeyore wandered into view from the side of the stable with a mouthful of sticks. He dropped them in the fire pit. Noticed me watching as he turned back to fetch more. He tried to smile, but the wrongness of its shape made my skin crawl. He said nothing, continuing from view again.

I tried my bonds. Firm. The edge of my paw found the ragged stub of a broken nail in the wood. Impossible to tell if it would help cut me loose until I tried, so I got to work while Eeyore was out of sight. "Piglet? Can you hear me?"

Not even a flicker. But I didn't think he was dead. Not yet.

I heard the donkey's shuffle before he appeared again, another load of kindling in his jaws. He dropped it in the pit and headed towards me on a straight line. I stopped work on my bonds. He smiled again, gaze fixed, glassy. He approached until he was snout to nose. He tittered. It sounded worse than the twisted grin looked.

"There appears to be a misunderstanding, Eeyore. I was simply asking Piglet–"

"I'm not as slow as I sound, Pooh." He sat back on his haunches.

"I had to try."

"I suppose it was only a matter of time before someone figured it out. Glad I didn't bet on who. I'd have lost the stable."

I bit my tongue. "Why did you do it?"

He eyeballed Piglet. "Everyone talks about all the flavors you get from pigs–loin and roast, ham and belly. I've always been curious. Maybe I'll put a little in the freezer until the hubbub over his disappearance dies down. See if I can get Rabbit to eat it before he catches on." His eyes were as mad as the rest of him. "After the barbecue, I'm going to kick you senseless again, drag you home, and hold your snout in a pot of honey until you suffocate. They'll find the note next to you confessing to Christopher Robin."

"Do you think you can duplicate my handwriting?"

"Do you think I don't know you're trying to cut your rope?" He bit a chunk out of my left shoulder and I screamed. The arm went numb. He shut me up with a head-butt. It shook the post to the rafters. I felt it in the vibration, the post's hollowness. I saw my chance.

It seems like the hard way always comes to the rescue.

"Why did you do it, you miserable ass? Why did you kill him?"

He continued dragging Piglet.

"I'm *talking* to you, you moth-bitten sack of woe. What's wrong? Run out of lies to tell?"

He stopped. Piglet's rope dropped from his mouth. "My tail."

"What about your tail?"

"That's why I did it. Do you remember when I lost my tail?"

"How can I forget? You mention how I found it every time you see me. If I develop dementia, your stupid tail is probably the only thing I *will* remember."

Color rose in his cheeks. His smile broke into a hard sneer as his voice lifted to a shout. "You found it, AND HE NAILED IT BACK ON! Christopher Robin took a hammer and a ten-penny nail and he drove the nail into my backside to pin the tail on the goddamned donkey! Did you know that's a children's game? All that time I thought he was being kind, he was MAKING FUN OF ME! Once I learned it was some people-game, it chewed at me, night after night, worse every time he came to the woods. I couldn't take it any more. So I lured him to the clearing and when his back was turned, I kicked and kicked and kicked until he was done. I left straw from Piglet's broom to muddy the waters if anyone nosed around."

My shoulder was on fire. There was worse pain coming. "And they say *I* have very little brain? He was helping you! What did they stitch up inside your head when they put you together–a family of inbred mice in a dirty sock?"

What's the expression people use? If looks could kill? He was close. One more push. So I shoved. Hard.

"And you're stupid enough to believe you're going to get away with it? On top of there being no mistaking donkey hoof prints for a broom, no one in their right mind would believe I'd die face-down in a honey pot, or lay a paw on Christopher Robin, you cock-eyed moron! Did that nail in your tail perforate your smarts, too?"

He brayed before he charged. Or shouted his name. It was hard to tell. He ran at me with as much speed as he could build in the short runway, dropped his head and drove it into my gut. Being roly-poly paid a small dividend, but didn't keep the wind in me when he hit. Winding him up did what was needed: the old post behind me broke with the impact. He retreated, out of his mind and intent on another run. I wheezed, fought through the breathlessness and the pain of the shoulder bite, and struggled to

get my bonds through the break. The rope popped free as he reached me. I tucked and rolled right. I wish Christopher Robin had been there to see me come up with my bound wrists in front of me. Eeyore struck the post again with a crack. As he backed up, I jumped and looped the rope around his neck.

I hissed. "An old jackass like you should have thicker skin."

He bucked and grunted as I strangled him. I might have finished the job, tried to, wanted to, until he smashed both of us through another post the ants or termites had long since hollowed out, and the stable loft crashed down on us.

7

"Pooh? Can you hear me? Pooh?"

I opened my eyes. "Piglet?"

"I'm here. I'm afraid I can't move, and I'm not sure why."

I had no idea how long I'd been out. Night was full and dark. No moon. "Eeyore tied you up."

"Over a broom? Pooh, I worry he's not entirely in his right mind."

Oh, Pork Chops–you have no idea. "Where is he?"

"I'm not sure."

I tried to sit up. Debris held me down until I shifted it off my chest. My shoulder screamed. The rope between my wrists had snapped. Eeyore might have bitten through it to escape. Impossible to tell in the dark. Logic said he was dead, unconscious, or gone in a hurry, or he'd have finished us both. "Where are you, Piglet?"

"Follow my voice," he said.

I found him shortly after, felt the knots, untied him. "You wouldn't happen to have a flashlight on you, would you?"

I heard him pat down his pockets. "How about that." A beam of light split the darkness.

I made a quick check of the rubble. No sign of Eeyore. Escape, then. Hundred Acre was a big place, but he couldn't run forever. I found the path away from the ruined stable. "We should return to your house."

"Why my house?" Piglet asked.

"It's closer. And has the benefit of not being here."

8

Eeyore couldn't even run for a day. At least that's what the tail in the Heffalump's clutch suggested.

"Found it down there by Murky Lake," he said. "In the mud along the shore." He held it in the end of his trunk. The nail, the literal point of contention, was still through the end of it, blood dried brown on its ten-penny tip. A light rain had begun to fall.

I studied the lake. "Were there any signs? Tracks in the mud, broken undergrowth or the like?"

He shrugged. "Didn't notice. Saw this, picked it up, contacted you. Doesn't look like it simply fell off. More like something took hold and ripped."

Had Eeyore come this way in an effort to escape and picked the worst cave to make a pitch for asylum? The Heffalump would never say, and knew I'd never ask. "What lives in Murky Lake?"

"Snapping turtles. Hundreds of them." He studied the tail. "Sure would have been stupid to wade in there."

"Eeyore wasn't blessed with an abundance of smarts."

He looked me over. "Huh."

"What?"

He shrugged. "They say that about you a lot, too."

"Is that some sort of threat?"

The Heffalump pulled his foot to his chest as if appalled by the thought. "Threat? My dear Mr. Sanders, it's a wish nothing bad happens to you."

"Like snapping turtles?"

He tipped his head towards my bite wound. "Like insane donkeys." He retreated for his cave, carrying his trophy tail.

There was a sour taste in my mouth as I walked home, the rain growing harder. It came from the sense of a job unfinished, despite knowing to my core the Heffalump had dealt with Eeyore, and with a severity far beyond yanking out his tail.

Did I envy the Heffalump his prize? What did it say about me if I did? It bothered me how I wanted so badly to end Eeyore. I could still feel the rope around his neck, his struggle, his fear before the stable crashed on us. It taunted me. Bothered me. More so because Christopher Robin would never have wanted to see me descend to a level on which I'd strangle the life out of anyone, no matter the cause–not even his own murder. He was a kind boy, a caring boy, and a wonderful friend who would have wanted me on the high road.

But I don't suppose that mattered much, not in the whole of Hundred Acre.

Christopher Robin was dead.

Sometimes finding a story is a game of Chutes and Ladders: you race up the rungs, leap a gap, miss another, tumble down a slide, land on square one again. In this case, only four words of the initial idea scrawled in a notebook remains in the finished tale. Along the way, it shed a paranoid boy who didn't like being followed and picked up two parole officers, a blue moon, and luckless career criminal Stu Conklin, who's old, tired, and almost ready to settle a decades-old score. Almost...

CUTTING

Edith, the younger nurse at the front desk of Verdant Gardens Center for Seniors, knows him on sight and offers a familiar smile. "Mister Pinkus. You're early."

Stuyvesant Conklin, who is not Mister Pinkus, signs the register with the name anyway. "The bus had somewhere else to be. I hope that's not a problem."

Edith fishes a visitor badge from the desk. "On the contrary, she's been asking for you this morning."

"Well, that's marvelous." He clips the pass to his sport jacket. It's not marvelous. It took three months of cold calling every senior living center and nursing home north of the city to find Mina Kobold, stashed under Pinkus' name; another three to establish himself as Pinkus in her failing mind. Conklin has no idea if Mina now asks for him, or in rare lucidity of thought asks for the grandson he impersonates. At least he can flip the brain card if she wigs out. *I don't know, Doc. One minute she knows me. The next, I'm some sort of pod person. It's tragic.*

Her room is bright when Conklin enters, curtains tied back to admit daylight. The space is impeccably neat; Mina spends most of her time in bed. She reclines there now, propped upright, a shrunken waxwork wrapped in a full-length plush robe of cobalt blue set off by fuzzy red socks. Her face is thin, her lips dull

and dry, her skin the tone of old china. Her gaze rests on the TV. Conklin doesn't know the talk show. Neither, he suspects, does she. "Hi, Nana."

Her eyes flicker from the screen. Her accent, undiminished despite decades removed from the old county, betrays Romania. "There you are, Bobo. You're late. Give your Nana a hug."

Conklin wouldn't have pegged Pinkus for a 'Bobo'. He hugs. Mina is old woman odors and the perfume failing to disguise them. "How are you today, Nana?"

"Meh. Better with my grandson, I think."

"They said you were asking for me."

"I was, but supper got cold."

He doesn't know what to do with that except feel bad for her confusion. "Sorry, Nana."

He makes small talk with her for a time, steers the conversation in fits and starts towards her long-ago home on Ardsley Road, finally hitting his script during a lull in conversation. "I'm afraid I've disappointed you, Nana."

"Oh, Bobo. You didn't mean for the fire to happen. My fault. It was more spell than you were ready for. But I won't tell your father. If anyone deserves the belt, it's me."

Conklin files *that* nugget of history away. "No, I mean about the book. Your–" he stops, exaggerates his glance into the hallway for effect, drops his voice by half. "Your little green book." He's only seen it once, decades earlier, a rare occasion Pinkus stumbled upon it inside the house. "You told me to bring it, but I couldn't find it where you told me. I looked, I swear, Nana."

"Where did I say to look?"

"In the compartment under the step up to the pantry, off the kitchen." Actually the place Pinkus kept lunch money from playground shakedowns when they were kids, but maybe it's detail enough to nudge her.

"I never kept it there."

"Where should I look?"

"Nowhere. It's here. Snug as a bug in a clearing. I'm not an old fool." She stops, the winds of the past spinning her pinwheel mind in a fresh direction, one with bite and spit. "Do you think I'm foolish? Stupid? You imagine I'd leave such knowledge behind, where it could be lost or taken? Or that I'd send a deceitful, vile little mole like you to fetch it? You're not to be trusted with it, not for one moment. Not after the fire you–" Her eyes open as if flames have blossomed between the end of the bed and the television. "No! What have you done, Bobo? Not a fire cast, never for one as inexperienced as you! You'll burn the house down! Run to the call box and pull it, now!"

She slips all the way into the memory. Conklin buzzes for an attendant as Mina sobs, chants, pantomimes motions designed to fight fire with elements decidedly different from water.

The attendant calms her with a mild sedative. "She's been doing so well the last few weeks, but these spells can come out of nowhere. Sadly, it isn't her first."

Conklin says nothing. His eyes have fixed on the bookcase in the corner: framed pictures of Mina's people, small mementos, and a dozen books, including an eye-catching title by Robert Frost. "Can I sit with her for a while?"

"Of course." The orderly finishes his task and retreats.

Conklin spends five minutes holding Mina's stiff, bony hand before crossing to the shelf. He removes the copy of Frost's IN THE CLEARING. Within its boards, most of the text block is missing, cut away to make a compartment for the battered bound notebook with pine needle green covers, snug as a bug.

Conklin's pocket proves an equal hollow for hiding it when he leaves. There's a pang of guilt, even though Mina's neither his kin nor responsibility. She deserved better than Bobo. They both did.

There are hundreds of spells in the notebook. Conklin focuses on two pages for a month before beginning the next phase.

-o-

"Pinkus will be at Elkhorn next Saturday night. Poker game with honchos from four other syndicates." The sound of five hundred hard-earned dollars sliding into Henry's pocket from Conklin's.

Conklin hopes the whiskey it buys is at least decent. "So eight days from now. Time?"

"Six p.m." Behind Henry, Conklin hears the IRT train, an

ambulance siren, maybe New York's finest as well. Busy night for a random corner in Queens.

"Entourage?"

"Dickey. Mutter. Maybe Chesky."

"I pay half a grand for 'maybe'?"

"Probably Chesky. Pinkus don't go upstate without him, on account of Chesky goes to Albany and the Finger Lakes a couple times a month, so he knows what's what."

"The money will be in your account tonight. Thanks, Henry."

"Don't do nothin' to get yourself sent back, Stu. You'd have to learn a bunch of new faces and associated crimes."

"I'll do my best." Conklin's been out again eight months. He's surprised he isn't already back inside. Groveland. Auburn. Coxsackie. He's been through all their gates. Maybe visiting Mina has kept him on the straight and narrow. *That* would be some magic trick.

"Maybe we grab dinner next time you're downstate."

"Sure thing. Take care." He hangs up on the lie.

With Henry settled, Conklin calls Ernie the Cobbler. Ernie's not his real name; Conklin uses a mnemonic device cooked from a combination of Grimm fairy tales and cookie elves from the TV commercials. "Remember those dance shoes we discussed?"

"Ayup."

"Will $500 put them in my hands by next Friday?"

Ernie doesn't even pretend to think about it. "Ayup."

"Pull the trigger."

"Ayup. Am I shipping?"

"No. These will be to go." He disconnects before Ernie can 'Ayup' again.

He takes a beer from the small fridge that came with the apartment. Parolee housing is better than a cardboard box, though the same shape and about as clean. He sits on the cot, pops the cap, sets his alarm for 8 a.m. for work–with all science has done, groceries still don't bag themselves–and puts on the Yankees game. He only half-watches. Doesn't know any of these kids. Wonders where quality guys like Willie Randolph have gone.

Eight days. Time always sounds bigger than it is.

Days pass with cans and boxes, bags and shelves at the market down the street. Nights between work and sleep, he continues to read Mina's spell book, committing words to memory as if the book might vanish in a puff of its own smoke, back to Robert Frost's clearing at Verdant Gardens.

Conklin calls his parole officer on Wednesday, alerts the man he's going out of town for the weekend. He feels twelve years old again, checking in with his mommy. It chafes. Everything does when you're sixty.

"Where to?" Conklin doesn't like his PO or the superior tone the man uses, even for two-syllable beats.

"Waterford."

"Still something there for you, Stu?"

"Reunion weekend." Neither hard truth nor soft lie.

"Uh-huh. Check in with–" Conklin hears key clicks. "Harry Whitbeck. Across the river in Troy. After you arrive and before you leave." Conklin takes down the number. "Keep your nose clean. I hear from anybody in Troop G, you'll be back in Groveland by Sunday supper." As if throwing State Police zones and prison names at him will leave welts.

Conklin packs light. A couple changes of clothes. Toothbrush and floss. A Zane Gray paperback he may have already read–after a while, all the sagebrush looks the same. A pair of black wool socks. A plastic zipper bag of pocket change. An ad hoc sewing kit. Mina's spell book. He debates the compact .357 he's not supposed to have, decides where he's going there will be a gun if he needs. He's surprised by how well he sleeps.

-o-

Friday morning, Conklin boards a bus for Albany. It's what he can afford after springing for information and new footwear. Danny's already letting him stay free in the apartment over his garage on Myrtle Street, near downtown. Danny got a different lie than Conklin's PO: funeral for a friend in Schenectady. He feels bad about lying to Danny. Danny's never rolled over on him, not once in forty years. Who deserves truth if not your pals and confidants? But Danny's also going to be out of town, so Conklin never has to look the lie in the eye.

Five hours on the bus. Half-full when it pulls out of Rochester, Conklin sits by himself the first three hours. The kid gets on in Utica and picks the empty seat next to Conklin. His t-shirt declares he's a SUNY POLY Wildcat–whatever the hell that is–established 1966. The kid tucks his backpack on the floor between his feet. He goes at a science textbook with a highlighter like it owes him money. The book lasts twenty minutes before boredom leads the kid to Conklin. "Going to Albany?"

"Christ, this isn't the bus to Allentown?"

The kid smiles too broadly for the quip. Great. A friendly one. "Tom Mix," he says, and offers a hand Conklin shakes.

"No kidding? Like the cowboy?"

"So I hear. I guess he was a big deal once."

"Yeah, but he should have stuck with one horsepower." The kid appears baffled. Conklin doesn't stop to explain. "Stuyvesant Conklin. People call me Stu."

"Nice to meet you. I suppose I'm a 'stu' too."

"Come again?"

The kid points to the t-shirt. "A student. Get it?"

Conklin realizes a sudden, crippling stroke would be more fun than two hours of this. "Yeah. That's a good one, cowboy."

"What do you do, Stu?"

"Time, mostly."

"I'm sorry?"

You will be, Conklin thinks. He considers praying the Litany of the Rap Sheet to the kid, the ins and outs of correctional facilities great and small across the last four decades, caught and released like a tournament bass. The truth of Conklin's life of crime is the punchline to the old joke: *But if I was good at it, I wouldn't have any friends on the force!*

Instead, he drops his voice to a murmur. "I'm on parole for a triple axe murder I committed thirty years ago. And I'm *seriously* considering recidivism."

SUNY POLY Tom understands big words and reads tone. He nods, his smile now smudged at the corners, and falls back into his book. Conklin drops his hat over his eyes and sleeps against the window. When he wakes outside Schenectady, the seat beside him is empty, Tom Mix vanished over the rise.

In Albany, Conklin buys a CDTA bus pass and a copy of the Times Union. He finds a payphone–landlines prove where he is–and calls his PO collect like a good boy. He repeats the trick for the local officer his PO named. Across the river in Troy, Harry Whitbeck uh-huhs and okays and gives the same advice as Conklin's PO about staying out of trouble. Conklin wonders if the same company that provides the cops with laminated Miranda rights also supplies warning cards to parole officers.

Suitcase in tow, Conklin deciphers the bus schedule and makes his way to Ernie the Cobbler's. The narrow storefront squats in an alley between two buildings on Central Avenue, grimy yellow paint peeling from the door in ribbons. He spends less time in the shop than he does finding it, leaves with a shoe box under his arm and his wallet another half a grand lighter.

It's two miles to Danny's garage apartment. It's a nice day, so Conklin uses it to break in his new footwear. The loafers are brown leather, hard-soled. Heavier than he imagined, but solid. Extra insoles from a drugstore add some comfort. He buys a meatball sub up the street from Danny's, and considers dropping into the adjacent liquor store for a bourbon nip. He talks himself past the place. Too much like planning a final drink.

-o-

Ensconced at Danny's, belly full, feet sore from working new leather, Conklin lays awake and stares at the squeaky ceiling fan. His mind navigates up the Hudson, into the Mohawk, all the way back to the headwaters on Ardsley Road when he and Pinkus were kids.

Pinkus had been small then, lean. What he lacked in size he made up in viciousness. The glow in his eyes was always a bit bright, a lighthouse warning of danger below the water. His smile came with a cruel twist at one corner. He'd bash, batter, or cut kids twice his size for slights. Hindsight tells Conklin he should have run the other way when they met in the third grade. For a moment,

Conklin can almost smell the asphalt playground the afternoon they first stood toe-to-toe and found a connection.

Pinkus was an ace at systems–cheats on tests, pocketing stuff at the five and dime, separating kids from their small change. Pinkus liked to have Conklin around because nothing stuck to Conklin. He walked with angels: never caught or blamed, always received the benefit of the doubt where teachers or cashiers– and later, cops–would have third-degree'd anyone else. Conklin couldn't explain it. He didn't think he was any more careful or less reckless than his peers. He simply never got singled out for punishment, and people who walked beside him seemed to enjoy a protective halo.

When Pinkus started his own syndicate–all of nineteen and at long odds to make it to twenty, given the people whose turf he was about to wedge himself into–Conklin was the first person he invited into the fold. They ran rackets the length of the north country, Saratoga south to East Greenbush. The money was especially big with the summer crowds of city slickers up from Manhattan for track season or the spa. Together they built slowly, made their names, got a little rich. It ran like clockwork for four years, right up to the night Pinkus went stray dog on Conklin–the night of the blue sturgeon moon.

Their outfit kept a private dock and warehouse along the Mohawk River for transferring merchandise. It was far enough from the Hudson to go overlooked, still close enough for give-and-take between Canada and New York City. Pinkus told Conklin a barge was coming down from Saint-Jean-sur-Richelieu with a load of knockoff cigarettes from a new seller, and Pinkus wanted Conklin's help verifying the shipment. Plausible enough. It all went south on the dock when three goons pinned Conklin to the boards on Pinkus' command.

"Nothing personal," Pinkus declared as Conklin struggled, the criminal's non-apology. "But I need what you have, and I can have it without you. Who doesn't want one less mouth to feed?"

A pair of silver sheers glinted in the shimmering moonlight. Pinkus rattled off something in a language Conklin had never heard, gripped Conklin by the ankle and SNIP SNIP SNIP along the outside of each foot, he cut off Conklin's shadow.

It bucked in the moonlight, a thin, man-shaped cloud fighting Pinkus' grip like some organized crime production of PETER PAN. He finally stuffed it into a Mason jar and screwed the lid on quick. He held it out for Conklin's uncomprehending gape. "It's like this, Stu. This shadow of yours is a sponge for bad luck. My Nana Kobold says some shadows work that way. Those people who skate through, always pick a winner, narrowly avoid the clink? People like you? Their shadows are personal lightning rods. Mine is so much blocked light. If I'm gonna move downstate, into Jersey and points south, I need the sort of cover your shadow provides. All I needed to take it was that beautiful blue moon up there. And to be honest, given enough time you might have realized your good fortune and gotten sweet on the idea of running the show yourself. I can't have that."

"You should kill me. You know I'll just come back at you."

"I wish I could, but I can't." He shook the jar and Conklin's detached shadow whipped within like a loose sail. "If you die, your shadow goes away. So you get to live, with only a small price to pay. But you should get out of crime. I suspect you're no good at it any more." The skinny little piss laughed at him.

They left Conklin on his back on the dock. His feet burned, though they were physically unscathed. Conklin thought the whole thing some weird brand of puppet theater until he noticed the full moon cast no shadow behind him. Twenty minutes later, a cop spotted him walking crookedly down the shoulder of the highway on account of the pain in his feet, questioned him extensively, and cited him for public intoxication for the hell of it. Three nights later, Conklin was caught setting an insurance fire a child couldn't have screwed up. So began the litany he'd withheld from Tom Mix on the bus.

For every backfired job that landed Conklin in a cell, Pinkus climbed another rung untouched by rival bosses and district attorneys alike. He moved downstate. Crossed into Jersey. It took time, but Pinkus now lays claim to a majority share of all the east coast action.

Conklin knows Elkhorn is the end of the line for one of them. As he drifts to restless sleep, he tries to ignore how history, experience, and shadow-play are all against him.

Conklin waits in a coffee shop, watches the front of Elkhorn. It's a converted brownstone just off Lark Street. Conklin only knows where it is because he's done his homework with tax records. He's assembled a mental map of the interior from Internet scraps: street and aerial views, old fire insurance maps, photos of the guts from a prior real estate listing. He even knows which room likely will host Pinkus' big-shot card game.

The house is quiet for so long past six, Conklin begins to wonder if Henry played him for a mark. Then the silver Bentley turns the corner and pulls to a curbside stop. Front doors open first. Dickey as wheel-man. Chesky riding shotgun. Mutter emerges from the back, street-side. All three have gotten older while Stu's been behind bars. They take in the sights before giving Pinkus the all-clear. The boss emerges. He's beefier, the once-skinny kid crammed to the rim with the good life. The trio surrounds him and the entourage enters Elkhorn.

Conklin checks his watch. Figures an hour for set-up and guests to arrive. Despite the absurd cost, he buys another coffee to avoid questions and keep his observation post. When the fourth player crosses the threshold, he makes his move.

-o-

Conklin leaps from the adjacent building's fire escape to Elkhorn's roof. He's almost a victim of his new shoes, slips when he lands, flails, nearly tumbles into the narrow alley between buildings–three stories down to a broken neck and cash-out of his bad luck account. Instead, his fingertips catch the remains of a TV antenna attached to the cornice work. The rusted bolts hold.

He works open the lock on an attic window using a pocket knife pushed through the rotted wood of the neglected sash. The open window is just wide enough to allow Conklin access. No alarm. For Pinkus, paranoia apparently doesn't extend to ninja action across rooftops. Within, the attic door is unlocked. The upper-most hallway is dark. A grab-bag of sounds filter up the stairs with the light from below.

Conklin discovers Mutter first, back to the door in a second floor room, counting money from satchels. The bills shuffle through the counter, masking Conklin's approach. When he's close enough, Conklin delivers pocket change upside Mutter's head via a black wool sock. Mutter bounces off the bill counter and slips from the chair. Conklin hits him again for good measure. He grabs a handful of restitution from the bill counter and crams it in his jacket pocket.

He chooses the back stairway to the first floor, moves with care down to the kitchen, pauses at the bottom, listens. Someone hums a tune. Has to be Dickey. Chesky hates music, enjoys humming even less. Conklin steals a peek around the corner.

Like Mutter, Dickey's back is turned. He's arranging cold cuts on a platter. Conklin recognizes the tune he hums, but damned if he can conjure the title. Before it drives him to distraction, he wallops Dickey behind the ear with the sock of change, catches the man before he falls and knocks things over.

Conklin spies the silver platter with two bottles of champagne and glasses, drink to go with deli. Hoisting it to hide his face, Conklin exits the kitchen in the direction of poker sounds.

As expected, Chesky is guarding the closed door to the salon where the game is, in a fashion unsurprising: planted in a chair, reading the digital racing form on his cell phone. The man never looks up. "Took you long enough. You and your chef d'cuisine nonsense. Clown. It's a frickin' deli tray."

Conklin sets the champagne on the small table flanking the closed door and draws his sock of coins. As he reaches back to cold cock Chesky, the man finally glances up from his phone, recognition and confusion fighting for his eyes. "Stu Conklin?"

The crack of the man's skull under the change sock almost sounds like "Yes."

There are two doors to the salon where the game is being held. Both are closed. The far door, the one Chesky wasn't watching, is closest to the front door. Conklin hears Pinkus within, holding court. The players won't want trouble. No poker pot is worth winning a bullet. And if you're a casual five card draw player who doesn't want to pay for your fun in blood or attorney's fees, you'll flee through the door closest to you, farthest from trouble.

Conklin retrieves Chesky's 9mm from the man's shoulder holster. He aims down the hall towards the kitchen. Shouts something inarticulate and fires two rounds. The 9mm is loud in the narrow space. He affects his best city accent. "Boss! Feds comin' in the back!"

The far salon door crashes open and four guys of various ages and ethnicities spill forth. They exit out the front like there's free money at the curb. Conklin closes and locks the front door behind them. He steps into the salon. Pinkus is at the other door, gleaming silver automatic clutched in his right hand. "Chesky, hold them off!"

Conklin sights him in. "Chesky's in dreamland."

Pinkus turns, sees the 9mm, goes from third gear to neutral. "Son of a bitch."

"Slurring my mother will only make this hurt more. Gun on the table. Slide it to the middle."

Pinkus complies. The automatic enriches the pot.

Conklin gestures to the chair nearest Pinkus, the 9mm a pointer. "Sit."

"Or what?"

"Or you'll fall down. Forever."

Pinkus sits.

Conklin presses the muzzle against the back of his head, handcuffs each wrist to a chair arm, and steps back. He studies the floor around Pinkus' feet. Counts five shadows. "You've built quite the collection."

Pinkus shrugs. 'What can I say, Stu? Yours worked so well, I stocked up every chance I got."

Conklin isn't sure which shadow is his until he walks in a circle around the chair. One of them shifts despite the light, follows him like a compass needle seeking north. "Inside left. That's where you attached mine."

Pinkus says nothing.

"Who do the others belong to?"

"Me. They all belong to *me*. And you couldn't take yours if you wanted to. I'm the only person left on Earth who knows how. Everyone else who knew is dead, and the instructions are in my head."

"Everyone?"

Pinkus spits at Conklin's feet to emphasize the point.

"Even Nana Kobold?"

"*Especially* Nana Kobold. Do you know how hard she worked to keep her magic from me? I had to learn the shadow spell from her little book on the sly. She kept finding new hiding places. All on account of one time, ONE time, a fire spell got away from me. Jesus, I was just a kid." Something in Pinkus' memory wields a fang. "She wouldn't give it up, and I got tired of asking, so I had her killed and dumped with a pair of concrete flats in Great Sacandaga Lake. Problem is the old bitch hid the book too well the last time. I did everything but tear the house down and still never found it. So if you want your shadow back? Tough tit."

"I'm surprised you had the stones to do it."

"Are you going deaf, Stu? I didn't say I killed her. I said I had her killed. I had Dickey do it."

Conklin understands now why Mina wasn't at Verdant Gardens under her own name: Pinkus hadn't stashed her there. Dickey had, in a fit of conscience. Probably on his own dime and under the only name he knew to use. Then he told Pinkus the job was done. Conklin almost feels bad for walloping the guy. "Did you actually see her body?"

"You saying I can't trust Dickey?"

"No. I'm saying Nana was better at the game than you. *Bobo*." He draws the old notebook from his jacket pocket like a deadly weapon or well-worn ace.

Pinkus' face discovers new shades of white, then red. "Bullshit! Bullshit that's my Nana's!"

Conklin opens it to a random page and shows him.

Pinkus huffs. "Where in the holy hell did–"

"Magic trick." Conklin interrupts. "For my next, I need a volunteer with multiple shadows. How fortunate you're here."

Pinkus moves as if to stand, ready to bring the chair with him. He stops when Conklin thumbs the hammer back. Settles. "You need a blue moon for the capture spell to work, genius. Next one is in seven months. And if I die with these shadows attached, they all go with me. Either way, you lose. Let me go now, and I'll make it quick for you."

"You always were a lazy student. That's why you had to cheat in school."

"Come again?"

"You need the light of a blue moon to *take* a shadow. But if you'd flipped the page, you'd know it can return to its rightful owner any goddamned time it wants. It just needs to be cut loose."

Conklin steps to the chair, grabs Pinkus' right ear and twists as if it might come off. Pinkus opens his mouth to scream and gets the balled-up mate to the change-filled sock jammed in for his trouble. Conklin kicks the table leg with his right foot. SNAP, and a razor-sharp blade pops down from the sole. The shoe resembles the bastard child of a loafer and an ice skate.

Conklin aims the shoe down the inseam side of Pinkus' left leg with minimal finesse. The blade slices through Pinkus' pants, shaves from mid-calf to the side of his foot. Conklin thinks of Dickey and cold cuts. Blood pools on the floor. The balled sock provides appropriate muffling.

Conklin stomps with the blade again. His shadow glides free from Pinkus, the edge of attached flesh inadequate to hold it. For a moment, Conklin fears it will flee the room, make the entire effort pointless. Instead, it curls around his legs once like a needy cat before rushing up his jacket sleeve. He feels it nestle in his armpit.

"That's us square," he says. Pinkus writhes, eyes of hate and grunts of rage until Conklin adds, "but it would be selfish to not consider the other three guys you screwed the way you did me."

He goes to work where the next shadow is attached, remembering all the barred doors as he does, the time wasted in cells, the bad luck moments he could have avoided, until the second shadow slips away and whirls into the hallway. He continues to whittle at Pinkus' feet, frees the third shadow, the fourth. Pinkus is passed out when Conklin finally stops, the man's own shadow as still as he is. Passing out doesn't stop the blood.

Conklin retracts the blade with another kick. He leaves through the front door, closes it behind him. The other untethered shadows soar away, become one with the night. Conklin doesn't know to whom they belong, if they'll reattach on their own over time. Mina's spell suggested the possibility. Conklin's not willing to leave his to chance.

Two lamps and the overheard bulbs from the fan throw enough light in Danny's garage apartment for Conklin to work. "This will probably hurt me more than you," he tells his shadow. When it stills, the man-sized outline reminds him of a shooting target. It aligns itself, laying the correct edge of shade beside Conklin's own bare, ice-numbed right foot, as if it's been waiting for this reunion. Nana Kobold's book says there won't be much blood, and there isn't, but it's slow-going with the suture needle and the catgut–actual catgut, because old magic seldom bends to the new world.

Thirteen stitches later through flesh and shadow, Conklin knots the line and speaks the spell. The stitches dissolve into his flesh. His shadow re-adheres, and not just where sewn: it folds and contours in deference to the light, conforms to him, becomes a true shadow once more. In the hour before he turns in, Conklin moves every couple of minutes to watch its duplicate motion, ensure it's still there.

-o-

No Pinkus-centric headlines top the local news on Sunday morning. It proves nothing. Alive or dead, his boys would have hushed it up. If alive, Pinkus may someday come after Conklin, or may be dissuaded, wary of Mina's magic in Conklin's hands. If he bled out, Chesky will see an opportunity to run the show and dispose of his body. Mob disappearances are their own sorcery. Either way, Conklin sees no point in fretting away what remains of an old con's life over it; but he resolves to return Mina's notebook. If karma is a form of magic, it seems the proper spell to perform.

The bus home is primed to be Conklin's own personal hell–a university's worth of students hover, waiting to board–when the primped and salt-and-pepper coiffed fifty-something pauses beside the empty seat adjacent Conklin and asks if it's taken.

"Be my guest," he says.

She sits. "Going to Rochester?"

"Yeah."

"Same same." She eyeballs the kids approaching in the aisle. "How did you wind up in this nightmare?"

"Economics." He's straight with her about being an old ex-con, in and out a few times, hates how he can only get menial jobs, had to come east, meager funds for the trip. He omits the mystical parts. Too soon to alienate her. "Anyway, I took the bus."

"An ex-con. Parolee?"

"Yes."

"Are you considering recidivism?"

Conklin wonders if his gaze resembles Tom Mix's in the moment. "No. I think I've finally learned a new trick." The driver starts the engine, closes the doors. "If you don't mind my saying, this bus doesn't appear to be your scene, either."

"I needed to come here on short notice to see my granddaughter. On principle, I have too much respect for gravity to fly. The train schedule didn't work. Enter the diesel bus."

"You don't drive?"

"I could ask the same of you."

He shrugs. "No car. Ironic, considering a driver's license is the only thing I can get without a problem."

She cocks her head, a faint, madcap gleam in her eyes. "Does your life experience include getaway cars?"

"Excuse me?"

"Are you a skilled driver? I took the bus because I fired my driver last week. He was overly fond of his drugs. As his passenger, I was not. I don't believe in luck, per se, but it sounds like you could benefit from a better job, and I could avoid a tedious search for another driver. Perhaps you'd like to discuss a career change while we ride."

Conklin isn't sure, will never be sure, but for a moment he believes his shadow nods before he does.

—o—

TRIPLICATE THREAT

[EDITOR'S NOTE: The death of superhero Iron Vanguard threw open the drawers of his secret case files, containing first-person narratives of encounters with every super-villain he faced. Whether he planned to write a book in retirement or merely desired a personal chronicle, we'll never know. But recovery of these files from the curb outside his apartment provides new, fascinating insights into the exploits of Iron Vanguard and his hero contemporaries. A legal team is clearing select dispatches for release in advance of the publication of a more complete examination of this remarkable life, RUST IN THE BLOOD: THE UNAUTHORIZED AUTOBIOGRAPHY OF THE IRON VANGUARD]

-o-

From the Files of the Iron Vanguard
Los Angeles, CA - 1982

After you've done the hero shtick for a while, you get a feel for who the criminal culprit is before some high-ranking muckity-muck gets to the first twist in the story. Maybe you hear things and file them away. Maybe connect-the-dots is your thing. In any case, when authorities call me in, if I'm going to have the 'aha' moment it's typically three minutes into the case history. It's not the muckity-muck's fault, so protocol suggests you stifle the yawn or try to look interested while it unspools. It's rude to step on the punchline–especially in Los Angeles, where no cop is really Joe Friday–so I let Lieutenant Daiken go on.

Politeness is how you grow old without realizing it.

"...and even though the crowd saw the guy, and I mean multiple witnesses, even one gal with a video camera–she didn't catch jack with it, but let me tell you, those spell serious trouble for the future–despite them seeing him walk out with the thing under his arm and take off, when we caught up with him he had an iron-clad alibi. I mean, airtight. He was at Dodger Stadium for a day game, fifty people around him–bought them all hot dogs, if you can imagine..."

I nodded. I could imagine. Chavez Ravine was supposed to be nice in the springtime. Good day for baseball if the smog didn't have its dander up, and Dodger Dogs to boot.

Sixteen minutes, I let him detail all six robberies and the witness conflicts, all liberally peppered with his asides and observations and how he lacked dependable eyewitnesses and something about some Akira Kurosawa film I haven't seen, before I could no longer stand still.

"The Clonemeister," I interjected.

He cocked his head like I'd spoken German in a French patisserie. "The what?"

"Who. The Clonemeister. Real name: Heinrich Viktor. First popped onto my radar back east last year. Similar M.O.: spotted at robberies, no regard for hiding his face, always eluded pursuit, and ultimately had an alibi with witnesses to back him up. The word on the dark side is he's a scientist who's figured out how to duplicate himself. By my accounting, he's three identical people."

"And I thought actors were weird. Why would anyone want to do that?"

"Aside from Super Alibi Power? In Philadelphia and New York, it helped him make off with a half a million dollars cash, all-in."

Daiken whistled. "He shoulda stayed east. He was doing better there."

"How do you mean?"

I thought he might tap me with a billy club. "Haven't you been paying attention? I already told you. All he's done here is make off with old movie camera parts."

-o-

The Sage Archivist of Mars–who isn't actually from the angry red planet, but merely a massive Edgar Rice Burroughs geek–pored over one of the million books on his shelves. His was an impressive library. I live on the back of a postage stamp in Brooklyn with two paperbacks on the nightstand at any given time. SAM turned a decommissioned Carnegie Library into his home and office, living in a suite in the basement, working on the two floors above. A bunch of us had helped him move from the warehouse he used to call home. Tens of thousands of boxes of books. But try getting him to help you retrieve a crate from the docks and he's all tied up with his Dewey Decimals.

"Hmm," he muttered several times as he flipped pages and turned the photos of the stolen camera parts. "If I'm reading this correctly, it appears the parts belong to a Model D three-color Technicolor process camera."

"Pretend I know nothing about this, because I don't."

"That's unfortunate. It's a fascinating point in film history. Not as pivotal as the advent of magnetic sound, maybe, but the process was occasionally used to great effect in–"

"No time for the hundred-year rabbit hole, Sammy. Broad strokes. Pretend I also don't care."

"One of the earliest motion picture color film processes used three negative strips to produce the final color image, one for each primary color. It required a specially built camera with a prism to split the image from the lens into the component color parts."

"Okay, I'll cop. That's sort of interesting."

"From what he's stolen, I'd say he's got all the parts necessary to assemble one."

I glanced over the pictures from Daiken. They were so many

36

metal and glass puzzle pieces to me. "Why *this* camera? Is it special aside from this weird three-strip thing?"

SAM shrugged. "It's an obsolete process. Has been for decades. He could more easily buy or steal thousands of other, better cameras if that's his goal. The camera itself is valuable, but he didn't even go about the robbery in a sensible fashion if that's what he wanted."

"How so?"

"There's a complete specimen in Rochester, NY at the Eastman Museum. Why run around staging six robberies and have to build the thing when you can commit one crime and be done?"

I mulled. "Because there's three of him. Everyone needs the same number of turns as the thief."

-o-

Catching a criminal mastermind is never easy. It's not like they advertise where they hole up. Most of the time, that's caves, volcanoes, underwater bases, occasionally outside the atmosphere. It's easier to defend a place no one wants to go. And it's not like there's an atlas of villain lairs, though the Sage Archivist of Mars has enough slack time to do the legwork. I had to twist some arms, map some coordinates, and make a few educated guesses to figure out where the Clonemeister was nesting. When I finally added it up, it made perfect sense: his lair was in the abandoned Spectrum Cinedome 3, east of Torrence.

No one wanted to lend a hand, despite the disparity in numbers. After eight months, SAM suddenly needed to unbox his collection of Baroque humor. Blue Barrister begged off, citing copious paperwork–nothing new there, though he bristled when I suggested he change his name to Blue Lame Excuse. Ditto the Ocher Zip, Miz LaMayhem, and Big Tall Gaul. Even Logan Bunkin, Sidekick-For-Hire, took a pass despite cash in hand. Homework my muscular butt.

So I went to the Clonemeister's lair alone, one against three, wanting to make short work of him and get back to New York in time for the late local news. Which usually translates into being caught in the first booby trap I stumble into.

For the record, in a world where you prepare for the Rube Goldberg machinations of madmen who overthink the plumbing, nets are an underrated threat: loss of balance, disorientation, forces of gravity, bouncing, general inability to do much besides flop like a fish for the first minute or two, all in one easy-to-use device.

Also for the record, the net was right inside the front door.

-o-

The lair proper, where Clonemeister manacled me to a theater seat, was in screening room three. As SAM figured, the fully assembled and somewhat decrepit-looking movie camera was there, in front of the screen and lighted to beat the band. Clonemeister had made some obvious modifications: it was controlled via nearby console. Heavy-duty power cables snaked from points unknown to the pedestal on which it sat. All three Clonemeisters tinkered with the set-up while I waited for The Big Reveal. It seems like a Hollywood cliché, the criminal mastermind spoiling the whole plan because he's already counted the unhatched chicken of the hero's defeat. But clichés come from somewhere. In truth, villains share how the trick will be done because they think you're muscle crammed into tights and too stupid to suss out their genius. Sometimes, like cops telling stories, you need to wait. But it was going to be annoying. The three of them talked in a wheel, one after the other, around and around like the world's worst ode to boat rowing.

"Iron Vanguard! Did you

    "really believe you could

        "slip into my lair unnoticed?"

"Yeah. I was a dope. Walked right into your net. I don't suppose I can take it back?"

"Take

    "it

    "back?"

"Why the camera? Have you tried one of those new video rigs? Way more portable. And cops already hate 'em. Huge upside."

Three offset cackles. He wasn't going to need a master plan. The tripartite conversation was going to kill me on its own.

38

"I've discovered a
     "way to use this
         "piece of equip–"
I interrupted. "Could you at least pick a single representative
to taunt, threaten and explain things to me? I'm still jet-lagged, and
the whole three-mouth Monte thing is about to trigger a seizure.
I'm pretty sure that's not the demise you want for me."

Turns out they could, but it took ten minutes of argument.
None of him wanted to surrender their voice in the matter. The one
who finally acted as spokesman even struggled a little working a
solo. "We've discovered a way to... deconstruct what the camera
captures into... component parts, essentially dividing it into
thirds."

He signaled the Clonemeister manning the control console,
who flipped switches while the third version pointed the camera at
the last seat of the front row. The camera hummed and rattled. A
beam of harsh light flared from the lens.

The seat shimmered in the glow. It was a single seat; then it
was three things flickering atop each other: green, blue, and red
iterations of the seat, an overlay out of alignment. Flicker turned
to flutter before the chair came apart with a soft 'pop' and fell in
three colored piles of dust to the floor. It looked like someone had
dumped a case of open Pixie Sticks. The hum died as the camera
powered down.

The Clonemeister was so excited, he abandoned single party
representation again.

"Do you see, Vanguard?
     "I've invented
         "a disintegration ray!"
"Swell," I said. "Your mom must be so proud. If only you'd
cloned her too. She could dote on you all equally."

"We're going to use it
     "to extort protection from
         "every A-List Hollywood star!"
"But first we
     "need a demo reel
         "to show their people!"
The Clonemeister manning the camera pointed it at me.

Maybe it was the adrenaline, but something clicked into place, a way out that didn't include being turned to Technicolor dirt. "Yeah, yeah. They're huge on the sizzle reel in this town. Before you shoot this little snuff film, I want a word with the top dog. Which one of you is the real Heinrich Viktor?"

"Don't be

    "foolish. We're

        "all real."

"Okay. The original, then."

The Clonemeister behind the bank of controls spoke. "I am the original."

I looked him up and down. Shook my head. "No you're not."

"No? What do you mean, 'no'? Of course I am."

"You can't be." I shrugged. "The original has just that little bit... more."

"More?" He looked at the others, back at me.

"More intelligent. More handsome. More likely to have done the lion's share of cooking up this tasty disintegration ray."

"But we're all identical!"

I bobbed a head at the Clonemeister behind the camera. "You, maybe. I see the way you operate that thing. This is all you, isn't it?"

"I'm him," all three claimed in unison. Frowned. Glowered at each other. "No you're not. I am!"

The fisticuffs and scuffling followed. I watched them punch, pummel, kick, bite, and otherwise abuse each other for another ten minutes from the comfort of my seat, flexing my arms and back to stretch shackles to breaking. Best show I'd seen in a while. They were battered and exhausted by the time I scooped all three into their own net and hung them from the ceiling.

-o-

A quick search found most of the stolen cash from the East coast robberies in theater one. I called Lieutenant Daiken and directed him to the lair. He arrived with about twenty cops and carted the Clonemeister away. All three were still grousing about which of them was the original as they were led out, talking over each other. That was all gravy. I suggested they not load him into one van, but no one ever listens to the helpful hints. Whatever. They'd figure it out.

Daiken marveled. "Three on one. How did you manage it?"

"I appealed to his vanity. You have to be pretty self-absorbed to think you're man enough to be three guys. I used it to break them up." I watched the cops disconnecting the camera. "In a way, I suppose I *also* created a disintegration ray."

Daiken looked at me like I'd called him a dirty name and strolled away.

Sometimes it's hard being the only hero in the room.

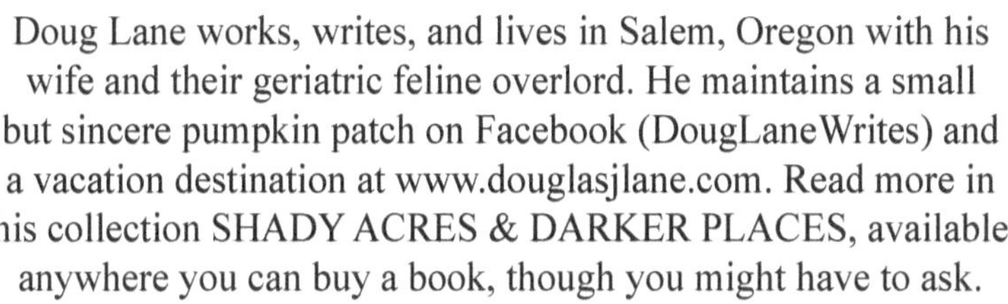

Doug Lane works, writes, and lives in Salem, Oregon with his wife and their geriatric feline overlord. He maintains a small but sincere pumpkin patch on Facebook (DougLaneWrites) and a vacation destination at www.douglasjlane.com. Read more in his collection SHADY ACRES & DARKER PLACES, available anywhere you can buy a book, though you might have to ask.

MIDNIGHT-TO-THREE
PUBLISHING